'It's not too late, Ebenezer,' the ghost of Jacob Marley wailed sorrowfully. 'Mend your ways!'

Marley was drifting outside as he spoke. Scrooge rushed over to the window and looked out. What he saw made his hair stand on end. There was a whole crowd of ghosts in chains, floating in the frosty air.

'Mend your ways!' they all moaned together.

Trembling, Scrooge slammed the window shut as hard as he could. 'I am a busy man,' he told himself. 'I have no time for this!'

Suddenly the bell rang.

Scrooge almost jumped out of his skin. He rushed into his office to hide, followed closely by Ellen the mouse. Meanwhile Gabriel watched, wide-eyed, from the safety of Scrooge's coat pocket.

Someone was coming up the stairs.

The doorknob was turning . . .

D1347515

Don't miss the other super tie-in to
this spectacular new animated film:

CHRISTMAS CAROL –
THE MOVIE
(PICTURE BOOK)

CHRISTMAS CAROL

THE MOVIE

Text by Narinder Dhami

CORGI YEARLING BOOKS

CHRISTMAS CAROL – THE MOVIE
A CORGI YEARLING BOOK: 0 440 864984

First publication in Great Britain

PRINTING HISTORY
Corgi Yearling edition published 2001

1 3 5 7 9 10 8 6 4 2

Set in 12/15½ pt Palatino
by Phoenix Typesetting, Ilkley, West Yorkshire

Corgi Books are published by Transworld Publishers,
61–63 Uxbridge Road, London W5 5SA,
a division of The Random House Group Ltd,
in Australia by Random House Australia (Pty) Ltd,
20 Alfred Street, Milsons Point, Sydney, NSW 2061, Australia,
in New Zealand by Random House New Zealand Ltd,
18 Poland Road, Glenfield, Auckland 10, New Zealand
and in South Africa by Random House (Pty) Ltd,
Endulini, 5a Jubilee Road, Parktown 2193, South Africa

Made and printed in Great Britain by
Cox & Wyman Ltd, Reading, Berkshire

Contents

Chapter One
Mr Dickens

1867. Boston, USA

It was a cold December night, and the streets were white with snow. A horse-drawn carriage was making its way down the main street, which was bustling with people. The biggest crowd was outside the theatre, and that was where the carriage stopped. People started whispering to each other, looking excited, and the theatre manager, Mr Gillman, rushed over to open the carriage door.

'Good evening, Mr Dickens!' Mr Gillman beamed as people stared at the famous man. 'This is a great honour!'

Charles Dickens climbed out of the carriage, and they shook hands. 'The honour is all mine, sir.'

'My apologies for our winter weather,' Mr Gillman went on, looking at the snow swirling down around them. 'Does it snow in England, sir?'

'Indeed it does,' Dickens laughed. 'I remember as a child being up to my neck in snow. But, of course, in those days I didn't have a beard to keep me warm!'

Neither of them noticed a little mouse snuffling around in the gutter near their feet. The mouse looked up at the poster of Dickens, stared at it for a moment and then scuttled off again.

The theatre was full to bursting with people who'd come to hear Charles Dickens speak. Everyone was chattering and laughing, and there was an air of great excitement in the audience. But as soon as Mr Gillman stepped out from behind the curtain, everyone fell silent immediately.

'Ladies and gentlemen, please welcome Mr Charles Dickens!' he announced.

There was loud applause as Dickens walked onto the stage. Nobody saw the mouse scurry out from behind a chair, then jump out of the way when someone nearly kicked him.

'Ladies and gentlemen,' Dickens began, 'it's really cold here tonight, but your welcome

8

has been most warming. Tonight I'd like to entertain you with a story of Old England. A story of *ghosts*—'

'Aaaargh!' A woman in the front row screamed loudly and jumped up from her seat. 'A mouse!'

Everyone in the audience stared.

'A mouse!' the woman screamed again.

The mouse had disappeared from view, but suddenly he scuttled out from underneath the woman's dress. She grabbed her husband round the neck, still screaming. The mouse was just as frightened as the woman. He scurried towards the stage, and disappeared out of sight down a crack.

Charles Dickens laughed. 'I've just been upstaged by a mouse, ladies and gentlemen!' he announced, his eyes twinkling. 'Let's hope I can make my story just as exciting.' He thought for a moment. 'I could start my story, too, with a mouse. A mouse making its way through London Town . . .'

Chapter Two
Ebenezer Scrooge

It was a cold, biting winter for the mouse, running through the snow-covered streets of London. A winter that was as cold for the rich as it was for the poor.

But the rich went about their business, warming themselves with promises of profit. One of them was the wealthy money-lender, Ebenezer Scrooge.

Scrooge was in the Royal Exchange, doing business with Mr Leach. Leach looked uneasy as he handed over a large portfolio containing the names of people who owed him money.

'Are they the ones I requested?' Scrooge demanded coldly.

'Yes, the accounts I agreed should be transferred to you,' Leach muttered.

Looking satisfied, Scrooge handed over a money order in payment.

'A sorry state of affairs,' Mr Leach sighed.

'Nothing, sir, that cannot be resolved,' Scrooge snapped. 'Good day.'

He marched off, leaving Mr Leach staring after him in disgust. 'Ebenezer Scrooge,' he muttered. 'Humph!'

Meanwhile, the poor made do with what little they had. At the Alms Hospital for the Poor, the sick children were lying listlessly in their beds, while their nurse, Belle, moved quietly round the room. One small boy was amusing himself by hanging upside down from his bed, when he suddenly spotted something small and brown running across the floor.

'Look, everyone!' he yelled. 'He's back! Gabriel's back!'

'Yeah!' The other children sat up, looking excited. 'Gabriel's back!'

Everyone jumped out of their beds, and knelt down on the floor. Gabriel the mouse beamed at his old friends, and promptly did a back flip, landing neatly on his small pink paws. The children laughed and clapped.

Flip! Gabriel tried another backwards somersault, but this time he landed inside a nearby slipper. Laughing, the children picked the slipper up, and put it gently on the nearest bed.

'Here, Gabriel, we kept this for you,' said the boy, handing the mouse a tiny piece of bread. 'We knew you'd come back . . .'

Ebenezer Scrooge was hurrying through the streets of London. All around him were street sellers, offering their wares – pots and pans, firewood and tobacco – but Scrooge ignored them. He had no time for such things.

He turned off the noisy, bustling street down a dark, lonely lane. It was narrow and dirty, the run-down houses packed tightly together. There was no-one about, and suddenly, for some reason he couldn't explain, Scrooge felt nervous.

What was that? Scrooge froze in his tracks.

His heart pounding, Scrooge looked round. He almost jumped out of his skin as he heard a loud cackle of laughter. 'Who's there?' he called out sharply.

'Mr Scrooge!'

Scrooge gasped with relief as a man with a hard, greedy face stepped out of the shadows. 'It's Old Joe.' The man grinned. 'It's

12

a pleasure to be of service to you again, sir.'

'I've just got these from Leach.' Scrooge handed over the portfolio. 'A full day's work for you here, Joe.'

Old Joe cackled again. 'It's as good as done, sir.'

Scrooge set off again through the mist. He stopped for no-one, not even a blind beggar who was standing in the street with his dog. The beggar rattled his cup hopefully as Scrooge went past, but he pushed them roughly aside.

'Beggars and dogs and street salesmen are like this confounded snow,' Scrooge muttered furiously. 'If it won't melt away, it must be swept away . . .' He hurried on.

'That's what Marley would have said,' Scrooge continued as he reached his office. 'Jacob Marley. My partner. My loyal friend.'

Scrooge walked up the steps and looked fondly at the brass plaque on the wall. MARLEY & SCROOGE. He took out his handkerchief and polished Marley's name. Then he went in and slammed the door shut.

Chapter Three
The Letter

Scrooge went into the office, where his assistant, Bob Cratchit, was hard at work. Cratchit, round-faced and cheerful-looking, wore several layers of clothes because it was so cold. Scrooge didn't allow a fire in Cratchit's room.

Without so much as a greeting, Scrooge hung up his coat in his own warm office. As he did so, he noticed a little mouse sitting on his desk, watching him. Scrooge's hard expression softened immediately. 'Ah yes, my assistant!'

Ellen the mouse watched eagerly as Scrooge reached into his pocket and produced a piece of cheese. But when he saw Cratchit glancing up from his work, Scrooge hesitated. He did not offer the mouse the cheese until his assistant had turned away again.

'That's enough payment, I'm sure you'll

agree!' Scrooge chuckled as Ellen grabbed the cheese eagerly. Then he sat down and began looking through his account books.

Meanwhile Old Joe, along with two bailiffs from Fleet Prison, was on his way to arrest everyone who owed money to Scrooge, and couldn't repay it. The wagon rumbled along a narrow street, and stopped outside a tumble-down house. The two bailiffs jumped out, and kicked the door in.

'Simon Speck . . . Jonas Buckle!' one of them boomed. 'We have a court order to take you to Fleet Prison!'

They threw their prisoners into the wagon as Old Joe looked on gleefully. Ebenezer Scrooge, the old skinflint, was going to be very pleased with their day's work.

Over at the Alms Hospital, one lucky boy was going home for Christmas. It was Tim Cratchit, whose father worked for Scrooge.

'Home, boy!' Dr Lambert said, popping a warm cap on Tim's head. 'No need to keep you here!'

'And look who's come to say goodbye,' Nurse Belle added.

Tiny Tim smiled when he saw Gabriel. He roared with laughter as Gabriel ran up his arm, jumped onto his head and did one of his famous back flips.

'We'll miss you, Tim,' Belle said, taking Gabriel and putting him gently on her shoulder.

Dr Lambert turned to Mrs Cratchit as Tim struggled with his crutch. 'He can go outside, but keep him warm. We don't want him to get that cough back.'

'Thank you, Doctor,' Mrs Cratchit said gratefully, handing him a coin. 'Thank you, Belle.'

'And Gabriel!' Tiny Tim added, smiling at the mouse.

'You're welcome, Mrs Cratchit,' said Dr Lambert. When they'd gone, he put the coin down on the table with a sigh. 'This won't go a long way.'

'Times are hard, Doctor,' Belle pointed out quietly.

'If only Mr Leach would see it that way,' the doctor groaned. 'We're weeks behind, Belle!'

'Mr Leach is a good man, Doctor,' Belle reminded him. 'He knows the work we're trying to do here.'

16

'I hope you're right,' Dr Lambert muttered.
Bang! Bang!

Someone was hammering loudly on the door. Next second, the two bailiffs burst into the room.

'Doctor Lambert?' the first bailiff snapped. 'We have a court order to take you to Fleet Prison!'

The doctor looked helplessly at Belle as the bailiffs dragged him away.

'Wait!' Belle cried. She ran out of the room, forgetting about Gabriel, who leapt off her shoulder onto the table. 'How can you do this? We have very sick patients.'

The bailiffs took no notice, and began pushing Dr Lambert into the wagon with the other prisoners.

Gabriel felt very scared. What was happening? Hearing heavy footsteps in the hall, he dived off the desk and onto the chair out of sight.

Old Joe came into the room. He had seized the opportunity to sneak into the hospital and nose around. Now he was looking for whatever he could find.

The coin was still lying on the table. Joe quickly pocketed it, much to Gabriel's disgust. Then he went over to the other door and opened it.

The door opened into the ward. All the sick children sat up in their beds and looked to see who it was.

'BOO!' Old Joe roared, pulling a horrible face.

Terrified, the children dived under their blankets, screaming and crying. Old Joe thought this was hilarious. Chuckling loudly, he went out again, while Gabriel glared at him.

'If you want him back, lady, you'll have to pay his debt,' the bailiffs were telling Belle. 'Until then, he's ours!'

Belle tried not to cry as she watched the wagon roll away. There was only one thing to do. She would have to go and see Mr Leach immediately . . .

Mr Leach looked rather uncomfortable when he found Belle on his doorstep. 'It is out of my hands, madam,' he muttered, when she explained what had happened. 'Your debts have been transferred to the offices of Scrooge and Marley.'

'*Ebenezer* Scrooge?' Belle turned pale.

'And you can expect no sympathy from *him*, madam,' Mr Leach went on, closing the door. 'I'm terribly sorry.'

'Ebenezer . . .' Belle murmured. 'After all these years . . .'

Back at the hospital, the children were asleep. Belle sat down with paper and pen, and began to write. She had an idea. It had to work. It must . . .

'*My dear Mr Scrooge*,' she murmured, then stopped. 'No . . .'

Gabriel had been having a nap in an old slipper, but now he skipped over to the table to see what Belle was doing.

'*Dear Ebenezer, it has been many years since I saw you . . .*'

'Squeak!' Gabriel jumped out of the way as Belle screwed up the letter and threw it onto the floor next to him.

'*Dear Ebenezer*,' Belle began again. '*It has been many years since we last met. And that occasion was not a happy one. But I write to you now in my hour of greatest need . . .*'

Chapter Four
Gabriel in Trouble

It was freezing inside the offices of Scrooge and Marley. Cratchit was so cold, he'd sneaked into Scrooge's office to warm his hands at the stove while his boss was out. Ellen the mouse wasn't too pleased.

Suddenly the sound of footsteps sent Cratchit rushing back to his own chair. But it wasn't Scrooge, as he had feared.

Belle stood in the doorway. 'I'd like to see Mr Scrooge, please.'

'He's out, I'm afraid,' Cratchit replied. He didn't notice Gabriel on Belle's shoulder, hidden by the folds of her shawl.

Belle walked into the office. 'I can wait.'

'I'm sorry, madam,' Cratchit said apologetically, 'but are you on our books?'

'Well, yes,' Belle admitted. 'But I *had* hoped to speak to Mr Scrooge personally.'

'You can't get out of the contract, you

know,' Cratchit said, looking uncomfortable. 'I can find the papers if you like.'

Belle looked round the office, her eyes sad. She saw ledgers, account books, a safe. So this was what Ebenezer Scrooge had become! 'Would you give this to Ebenezer, please?' she asked, taking the letter out of her purse.

'You mean Mr Scrooge?' Cratchit frowned as Belle turned and left. 'But he's a very busy man!'

As Belle hurried down the stairs, Gabriel leapt off her shoulder onto the handrail. The mouse was determined to make sure that Scrooge read Belle's letter, however busy he was. He dashed up the handrail towards the office, and saw Cratchit put the letter on his desk. Gabriel jumped down and scurried into the room, not knowing that he was being watched by another mouse hiding in the shadows . . .

Meanwhile, Scrooge was on his way back to the office. He pushed his way irritably through a group of carol-singers, and turned the corner.

The street was dark and gloomy, and there

was no-one around. Scrooge hurried up the steps of the office.

'Merry Christmas, Uncle!' called a cheery voice.

'Humbug!' Scrooge muttered.

'Strange words for Christmas-time, Uncle!' Scrooge's nephew, Fred, ran over to him. 'It's the only time of the year when all people, rich and poor, open their hearts to each other!'

'*And* the only time of the year when unwanted relatives make unwanted visits!' Scrooge snapped.

Fred's face fell. 'I just wanted to ask if you'd come to Christmas dinner with us tomorrow, Uncle.'

'I'll be busy,' Scrooge said shortly, going inside.

'Surely you don't work on Christmas Day, Uncle!' Fred chased him up the stairs. 'My wife and I would—'

'Why did you get married?' Scrooge interrupted him rudely.

'Because I fell in love!' Fred replied.

Gabriel, who was hiding under a book on the desk, peeped out to see what was going on.

'Love . . .' Scrooge muttered scornfully. He stared at his nephew. 'What do you want from me?'

Fred looked shocked. 'Nothing.'

'Delighted to oblige!' And Scrooge slammed the door in his face, making both Gabriel and Cratchit jump.

'Mr Cratchit,' Scrooge went on furiously, 'never marry!'

'But I *am* married, sir,' Cratchit began apologetically.

'Humbug!' Scrooge roared. 'Merry Christmas, indeed! He's as poor as a church mouse!'

Gabriel looked disgusted at *that*.

'Oh, sir, a woman came to see you today,' Cratchit remembered suddenly. 'A client.'

Scrooge wasn't listening. 'There!' he grunted crossly, slamming a large book down on Cratchit's desk. 'Attend to this!'

To Gabriel's horror, the heavy book sent Belle's letter flying into the air. It drifted to the ground, and lay there.

'Now where did I put it?' Cratchit mumbled, searching his desk.

He'd have to get the letter himself, Gabriel

decided quickly. It was much too important to leave lying around.

'Every fool who walks about with "Merry Christmas" on his lips should be boiled in his own pudding!' Scrooge muttered.

Gabriel began to climb down the desk. As he did so, the carol-singers stopped beneath the office windows, and began to sing heartily.

'Confound it!' Scrooge roared, stomping across the room.

Gabriel squeaked, and panicked. He lost his hold on the desk and fell . . .

Chapter Five
Marley's Ghost

Splash!

The little mouse plunged straight into a bucket of water which stood on the floor below him. He floundered helplessly for a moment – then, suddenly, a paw reached into the bucket towards him. Gabriel grabbed it thankfully, and was towed to safety.

Ellen flipped Gabriel out of the bucket onto the floor. Then she folded her paws and stared sternly at him. She wanted to know *exactly* what he was doing there!

Scrooge was glaring down at the carol-singers. Tiny Tim Cratchit and his brother Peter were amongst the little group, Tim holding a candle.

'Greetings, sir!' The choirmaster beamed at Scrooge. 'Your nephew asked us to sing for you!'

'We shouldn't, sir,' Peter Cratchit whispered nervously. 'Our dad works here, and—'

Scrooge was furious. He grabbed the bucket of water and emptied it out of the window over the carol-singers. 'Now be gone with you!' he roared.

The carol-singers were drenched.

'I'm all wet!' one moaned.

'What a scoundrel!' another said angrily.

'I'm freezing,' Tiny Tim whispered.

Gabriel could hardly believe his eyes. 'SQUEAK!' he roared at Ellen. *The man's mad!*

Angrily Scrooge slammed the bucket down on the floor, and Gabriel was forced to leap out of the way. Scrooge didn't see him, but he spotted Ellen, and held out his hand to her. Ellen looked smugly at Gabriel, and blew a big, fat raspberry at him.

Outside, Tiny Tim couldn't stop sneezing. He'd sneezed so hard, he'd blown his candle out.

'Best get your poor brother home out of the cold, Peter,' the choirmaster said anxiously.

In the office, Cratchit was listening impatiently to the clock ticking away. It was

Christmas Eve, and he wanted to go home. How much longer would Scrooge expect him to stay?

Scrooge looked up from his accounts. 'There's still much to be done before we lock up for the night,' he snapped.

'Yes, sir,' Cratchit agreed gloomily.

Gabriel saw that Belle's letter was still lying under Cratchit's desk. He began to tiptoe towards it. The mouse was halfway across the room, when suddenly—

'SQUEAK!' Ellen popped out from behind the door. *BOO!*

Gabriel got the fright of his life. He did a back flip, and landed under Cratchit's desk. 'Squeak!' he yelled furiously as he picked himself up. *Why do you keep picking on me?*

Ellen glared at him. 'Squeak!' *You can get out of here right now!*

'SQUEAK!' Gabriel pointed at Scrooge. *Not until I take this letter to him!*

Ignoring Ellen, Gabriel began tugging at the letter. It was too heavy for him, and he couldn't move it at all. Ellen shrugged, and tapped her furry head. *He's mad!*

Just then the church bell began to chime seven o'clock.

'I suppose you want me to pay you for tomorrow,' Scrooge muttered crossly. 'Two and six to stay at home and be idle!'

'It only comes once a year, sir,' Cratchit murmured. He reached for the money gratefully. 'Thank you, sir. And a merry—' He saw the look on Scrooge's face, and stopped.

'And I want you here extra early the day after, to make up for lost time,' Scrooge snapped as Cratchit left.

Ellen had decided that the only way to get rid of Gabriel was to help him with the letter. So she lifted one end of it, while Gabriel took the other. But the letter was heavy, and Ellen was struggling. 'Squeak!' she complained.

Scrooge looked up. 'What the—?' he began, puzzled. Gabriel just had time to hide behind the table leg as Scrooge hurried across the room.

'Cratchit!' Scrooge breathed furiously, spotting the letter. 'That good-for-nothing! Even a tiny mouse is tidier . . .' He grabbed the letter and put it in the pocket of his frock coat. Then he patted Ellen, who looked smugly at Gabriel. 'This must be the letter Cratchit was

28

going on about,' Scrooge muttered. 'Well, it can wait.'

Bong!

The clock had suddenly started to chime. Scrooge glanced at it and, to his amazement, he saw that the hands had begun to spin round. Faster and faster they spun, as the clock continued to chime. Then the pages of the book lying on the desk began to turn at speed, as if an invisible hand was flipping through them. The whole room was vibrating, as if a giant had picked the building up and was shaking it as hard as he could.

'Silence!' Scrooge shouted in a trembling voice as Gabriel and Ellen ran for cover in the stove. '*Silence!*'

Immediately everything stopped.

'I must go,' Scrooge stammered nervously. 'I'll be in early tomorrow . . .'

But it wasn't over yet. Scrooge stared round fearfully: a strange, blue light filtered slowly into the room. He could hear a frightening sound, too. The sound of heavy iron chains clanking and rattling as they were pulled along.

'*Ohhhh!*'

Someone was moaning at the window. As the blue light faded to a white mist, a head appeared. 'Hear me, Ebenezer!'

'Marley?' Scrooge recognized the voice of his long-dead partner. 'Is it really you?'

The misty outline of the ghost became a little clearer, and Scrooge saw that Marley was wrapped around with iron chains.

'I've come to warn you, Ebenezer,' Marley moaned softly.

The mice crept out of the stove to see what was going on. They were fighting for the best position, and Ellen kept pushing Gabriel out of the way, so he decided to find a better spot of his own.

'What's happened to you, Marley?' Scrooge stared in horror at the ghost. 'Who did this?'

'I did this,' the ghost moaned. 'These are the chains of my ignorance, Ebenezer!'

Gabriel scurried across the room and climbed up the coat-stand. He tucked himself away in the pocket of Scrooge's coat, where he could see and hear everything perfectly.

'But you were always a good man of business, Jacob,' Scrooge began.

'I wasted my days hoarding money!' Marley wailed. 'Listen, Ebenezer.' He fixed his gaze on Scrooge. 'You shall be haunted by three spirits!'

'Haunted!' Scrooge repeated, terrified.

'Expect the first when the bell tolls one,' Marley went on.

'Can't I see all three at once and have it over with?' Scrooge stammered. 'I'm a busy man, Jacob.'

'It's not too late, Ebenezer,' the ghost wailed sorrowfully. 'Mend your ways!'

Marley was drifting outside as he spoke. Scrooge rushed over to the window and looked out. What he saw made his hair stand on end. There was a whole crowd of ghosts in chains, floating in the frosty air.

'Mend your ways!' they all moaned together.

Trembling, Scrooge slammed the window shut as hard as he could. 'I am a busy man,' he told himself. 'I have no time for this!'

Suddenly the bell rang.

Scrooge almost jumped out of his skin. He rushed into his office to hide, followed closely by Ellen. Meanwhile Gabriel watched, wide-eyed, from the safety of Scrooge's coat pocket.

Someone was coming up the stairs.

The doorknob was turning . . .

Chapter Six
The Ghost Of Christmas Past

Trembling, Scrooge peered round the door as two gentlemen walked in.

'Good evening, sir,' said one of them. 'Am I addressing Mr Scrooge or Mr Marley?'

'Marley is long dead, sir,' Scrooge replied. 'Marley died seven years ago on this very night!' He laughed wildly to himself. 'Ha ha!'

'We're raising money for the poor, Mr Scrooge,' the second man explained.

Scrooge turned to pick up his coat. 'You're *real* gentlemen then?' he asked suspiciously.

The men looked puzzled.

'We like to think so, sir!' said the first man. 'How much—'

'Excuse me, gentlemen,' Scrooge interrupted him rudely, 'I must run.'

'Of course, sir,' said the first man, following

him over to the door and out of the office. 'How much are you happy to give?'

'Squeak!' Ellen gasped, realizing that Gabriel was still in Scrooge's coat pocket. She dashed over to the window. Scrooge had shut it so violently when he saw the ghosts that it had snapped open again a little way. Ellen peeked out, and saw Scrooge and the two gentlemen standing below in the snowy street.

'Have the workhouses closed down then?' Scrooge was asking scornfully.

'No, sir,' the second man was saying, 'but many of the poor would rather die than go to a workhouse.'

'Let them die then!' Scrooge retorted cruelly, and turned away. 'They can make themselves useful by decreasing the population!'

Ellen was determined not to be left behind. She launched herself out of the window, and sailed through the air towards Scrooge. She landed on top of his hat, but then she bounced off again, and slid down his arm towards the ground.

Gabriel could hardly believe his eyes when he saw Ellen sliding past him. He shot out his paw, caught her and dragged her into the pocket with him.

'Squeak!' Ellen said crossly, pushing Gabriel away.

Gabriel shrugged. *What was wrong with this mouse?!*

Cratchit was hurrying home to his family. The pavements were icy, and children were enjoying sliding around on them. Two boys slid along, whizzing past Cratchit and just missing him.

'Careful, now!' Cratchit called. 'We don't want you falling over!' Then, suddenly, his own feet seemed to slip from under him. 'Oh – help!'

He stumbled, slipped and began to slide along on the ice at great speed. 'I can't stop!' he yelled as he zoomed along the pavement, waving his arms about. *'Help!'*

The other passers-by watched in amazement as Cratchit skidded the whole length of the street. He only managed to stop himself right at the very end.

'Do it again, Mr Cratchit!' the boys laughed.

'Ahem!' Cratchit was bright red. 'You'll have to wait till next year!'

Smiling, Cratchit let himself into his house. His family were gathered round the stove, and Mrs Cratchit had Tim on her lap, wrapped in a blanket.

'Hello, Father,' called Rosy and Peter.

'Happy Christmas, Daddy!' Sara rushed over to hug him.

Cratchit smiled fondly at her. 'And a happy Chris—'

He was interrupted by Tiny Tim coughing hard.

'What now, Tim?' Cratchit rushed anxiously over to his son. Tim looked feverish and pale.

'He's only just back from the hospital, Bob,' Mrs Cratchit pointed out gently.

'We've got sugar sticks, Dad,' Tim said, still coughing.

'And sweets and wine,' Rosy added.

Cratchit tried to sound cheerful in spite of his concerns about Tim. 'Then we shall have the best Christmas ever!'

'Yes, the best Christmas ever!' Tim repeated, beginning to cough again.

Scrooge was unlocking the door of his house. He was tired and cold and frightened.

Would everything happen just as Marley had said?

Then Scrooge's heart began to pound with fear. The brass knocker on the door was glowing strangely. He stared at it, terrified of what would happen, but unable to tear his eyes away. The lion's head changed shape, and turned into the face of Jacob Marley.

'Mend your ways!' he moaned.

'Marley!' Scrooge gasped, clapping his hand over his eyes. Trembling all over, he rushed into the house, and bolted the door behind him.

'We ran an honest business, Marley,' he muttered wearily. 'Always did and still do.'

Scrooge went into the living-room. It was a dark, gloomy place, even when he lit the candles. He took off his coat and threw it on the sofa, tumbling the mice around inside the pocket.

Scrooge went into the kitchen and returned with a bowl of porridge. He trudged wearily into the bedroom and undressed, hanging his frock coat over a chair. He put on his dressing-gown and nightcap, then sat in front of the fire to eat his supper.

Meanwhile Gabriel clambered out of

Scrooge's coat pocket, with Ellen close behind him. He ran over to Scrooge's bedroom, and peeped in. There was Belle's letter, sticking out of the pocket of Scrooge's frock coat.

Ellen thought Gabriel should stop interfering: she grabbed his tail and hung on tight. They had a tug of war, which Gabriel won. He whisked his tail free, sending Ellen head-over-heels. Then he scurried into the bedroom and climbed up the sleeve of Scrooge's coat.

'SQUEAK!' Ellen ran over to Scrooge, and squeaked with all her might.

Scrooge looked amazed when he glanced down and saw her. 'How did you manage——?' he began.

'SQUEAK!' Ellen interrupted, pointing at his frock coat.

'In my coat?' Scrooge guessed. 'You *are* clever!' He placed Ellen and the bowl of porridge on the chair. 'Have some porridge. You'll be welcome company tonight.'

Ellen was almost dancing up and down with impatience. She couldn't make Scrooge understand her, however much she screeched. 'SQUEAK!' she yelled as she saw Gabriel pulling the letter out of Scrooge's pocket.

'What now?' Scrooge asked wearily.

Gabriel let the letter fall to the ground. As Scrooge glanced round, the envelope on the floor caught his eye.

'That letter again!' He frowned, bending to pick it up.

Ellen squeaked furiously, but Gabriel was delighted that he'd finally won. He jumped down onto the chair and lay on his back in the porridge, having a feast.

Meanwhile, Scrooge had climbed into bed with the letter. He ripped open the envelope, then yawned widely. 'I'll read it tomorrow,' he decided, tossing it aside.

Gabriel was dismayed. He climbed out of the porridge bowl and dashed over to the bed. But by the time he reached it, Scrooge was already snoring, Ellen sitting beside him.

Then it began . . .

Through the darkness, a bright, golden yellow flame appeared. The flames flickered and grew in brilliant shades of green, shaping themselves into the face and figure of a ghostly child. She was holding a cone under her arm.

The mice were terrified. Gabriel jumped

into the pocket of Scrooge's dressing-gown, and Ellen dived out of sight under the letter.

Scrooge opened his eyes. 'The haunting has begun!' he moaned, his voice full of dread. 'Are you the spirit?'

'I am the Ghost of Christmas Past,' the girl said softly.

'Long past?' Scrooge asked falteringly.

'No,' the ghost replied. '*Your* past, Ebenezer Scrooge.'

Scrooge shaded his eyes from the brightness with a shaky hand. 'Could you turn off the lights?'

The ghost smiled. 'I am here to light your past.'

'Well, I'm not interested, thanks.' Scrooge lay down again and closed his eyes. 'I'd rather have a good night's sleep . . .'

The glowing light travelled swiftly round the side of the bed. Scrooge opened his eyes again to find the spirit standing right next to him. 'Aargh!' His scream of terror made Gabriel and Ellen cry out too.

The ghost girl held out her glowing hand. 'Walk with me!'

Scrooge was afraid to touch her, but the spirit drew him out of bed against his will and

40

led him over to the window. Meanwhile, Ellen crept out from beneath the letter to see what was going on.

'But I am a mere mortal!' Scrooge spluttered. 'I cannot pass through walls like a spirit – aaargh!'

The ghost reached out and lightly touched Scrooge's chest. There was a flash of light, and next second they were drifting towards the closed window.

As the spirit guided Scrooge through the glass, Ellen made a desperate bid not to be left behind. She leapt from the bed and made a grab at Scrooge's slipper as his feet passed through the window. She missed and hit the cold windowpane, crashing down onto the sill. Gabriel was still in Scrooge's pocket, and she'd been left behind . . .

Chapter Seven
Young Ebenezer

The ghost held Scrooge's hand as they flew over the snowy rooftops of London. Gabriel had got over his first fright, and was now enjoying himself as they glided through the air.

'Do I know you?' Scrooge asked the ghost curiously.

The girl smiled. 'Yes, but you've forgotten. Look . . .'

A bright stream of light suddenly poured out from the cone under the ghost's arm. The dark, snowy, winter's night was gone. Instead they were drifting above the countryside on a bright spring day. Below them, three boys were cantering along on their ponies.

'Why,' Scrooge gasped, hardly able to believe his eyes, 'that's Tom and Stanley! I know these boys, but surely now they must be men . . .'

'They are shadows of things that have been,' the ghost explained. 'We can see them, but they cannot see you!'

They flew away again.

Soon they left the bright spring countryside behind, and drifted through clouds into a dull, grey and dismal place. A large, ugly building stood on a hill before them.

'I know this place,' Scrooge muttered bitterly. 'I was at school here . . .'

The ghost glided towards the heavy wooden door, taking Scrooge with her. They passed straight through it, into the grim-looking building.

They were inside a big, dark dormitory. Uncomfortable-looking beds were pushed against the walls in rows, and on the furthest bed sat a young boy. He looked desperately sad.

The door opened, and a hard-faced schoolmaster walked in. 'Well, Ebenezer,' he said harshly, 'I don't expect anyone will come for you now. Ha ha!' He laughed heartily. 'Well, Merry Christmas anyway!'

Tears rolled down the boy's face as the schoolmaster strolled out. Gabriel couldn't help sniffing and wiping his eyes too.

'My father was a difficult man,' Scrooge tried to explain. 'I did not understand back then . . .'

The ghost looked grim and nodded. 'Let's see another Christmas.'

She began to spin, throwing out autumn-coloured leaves in all directions. Then the room began to swirl with snowflakes. It changed to spring, then to summer, and back to autumn again. Three times the ghost spun her way through the seasons.

Then, slowly, the room settled down again. They were in the same grey dormitory, and a pretty young girl was running towards them. 'Ebenezer?' she called.

Scrooge turned, a smile transforming his face. '*Fan?*' he said in disbelief.

'Ebenezer!' Fan rushed past Scrooge's outstretched hands towards the boy. He was still sitting on the same bed, but he was now three years older. 'I've come to take you home!'

'Home, Fan?' Young Ebenezer gasped.

'Yes, I asked Father and he agreed!' his sister replied joyfully. 'We'll have the merriest Christmas ever!'

Scrooge could hardly bear to watch.

'You are to leave this place for ever, Ebenezer!' Fan went on.

Smiling, Young Ebenezer picked up his bag, and he and his sister went out. Scrooge watched them tenderly. A large tear rolled down his cheek and splashed onto Gabriel's head as the mouse watched too.

The grim schoolmaster was waiting at the door to see them off. The two children stepped outside into brilliant sunshine and walked to the waiting carriage. Scrooge and the ghost glided after them.

'Ebenezer,' Fan beamed, 'meet my dearest friend in the whole world!'

A sweet-faced girl was waiting for them in the carriage. She smiled shyly at Young Ebenezer.

Scrooge turned white with shock. 'Belle!' he gasped.

Young Ebenezer leaned over to shake hands with his sister's friend. The handshake went on for quite a while, and Fan smiled to herself. She'd hoped Belle and her brother would like each other . . .

The driver cracked his whip, and the horses trotted off.

'Do you remember?' the ghost asked quietly.

'Yes.' Scrooge nodded sadly.

Gabriel looked confused. What was happening?

Swiftly the scene changed, and they were now flying straight towards a large, important-looking mansion.

Scrooge looked puzzled. 'Why are you taking me home?' he asked.

The ghost didn't answer. She simply guided Scrooge into the house. Young Ebenezer was waiting in the drawing-room with Fan and Belle. He looked very nervous.

'Ah, there you are.' Scrooge's father strode into the room and stared sternly at his son. 'When you left this house you were an untidy, badly-behaved boy. I have spent a great deal of money on your education.' He looked Ebenezer up and down. 'Has that money been well-spent?'

'I hope so, sir,' said Young Ebenezer hesitantly.

'Have they taught you a good under-standing of figures?' his father demanded.

'Yes, sir.'

'Well,' his father went on, 'we'll see

whether you will be any use to this family or not. You will leave for London tomorrow to work at Fezziwig's, and you'll send home half your wages . . .'

The ghost pulled Scrooge after her, as they glided away from the scene.

'My father's respect had to be earned,' Scrooge muttered uncomfortably as they flew out of the house. 'But I know he would be proud of me if he were alive today!'

Again the ghost didn't answer, but her lips tightened and her face grew older and wrinkled as she looked at him.

Within a few seconds they were back over the rooftops of London again, swooping down to a bustling street.

Scrooge's face lit up. 'Fezziwig's!' he exclaimed.

They entered the building through the wall. They were in a large office, warmed by a roaring fire which crackled in the grate. A moment later, the clock began to strike.

'No more work tonight!' Fezziwig, a plump, cheery-faced man, bounced up from his chair. 'It's Christmas Eve! Come on, Ebenezer, let's make ourselves a ball-room!'

47

As Young Ebenezer helped his boss move the desks, Scrooge smiled. 'Old Fezziwig, alive again!' he muttered softly.

Gabriel had popped out of Scrooge's pocket to see what was going on. Suddenly he noticed the ghost staring at him and, alarmed, he dived out of sight again. But the ghost only smiled although now, he noticed, she looked young again.

A crowd of people had arrived for the party, and were being greeted cheerfully by Fezziwig.

'Merry Christmas, everyone!' he called. 'Ebenezer, your sister's here – with Frederic! How are you, lad?'

'I remember *him*!' Scrooge said bitterly. 'Much as I'd like to forget him – the rogue!'

'You were expecting someone else?' the ghost asked quietly, her voice sombre and hoarse.

'Yes.' Scrooge looked embarrassed. 'She was a good friend of my sister's. Belle was her name.'

Gabriel gave a screech and nearly fell out of Scrooge's pocket.

'But she came from a poor family,' Scrooge went on, 'and I believe her father drank . . .'

The ghost's face suddenly shrivelled and aged as she turned to him in disappointment.

The party was getting underway now. A band began to play, and couples danced, while others enjoyed the delicious food. Belle arrived, looking prettier than ever, and was greeted warmly by Fan and Young Ebenezer. Gabriel clapped along happily to the music as Young Ebenezer and Belle danced together.

'That old Fezziwig!' Scrooge smiled. 'He truly was a gentleman.'

'He spent a little money on a party,' the ghost said. 'Does that make him a great man?'

'It was *more* than that!' Scrooge snapped. 'He knew how to make our work a pleasure—' He stopped himself from saying more.

The party at Fezziwig's was over. Young Ebenezer and Belle were sitting together in the carriage, while Fan and Frederic ran about in the street, throwing snowballs at each other.

Belle smiled. 'Fan is so happy!'

'We'll be even happier, Belle,' Young Ebenezer replied. 'I'm saving up.'

Belle frowned. 'Money isn't all that matters, Ebenezer.'

'Belle, I want you to have *everything*,' the young man told her firmly.

Belle smiled again. 'All I would want is to dream of you, Ebenezer!' And she kissed him on the cheek.

The ghost's face darkened and grew even more wizened. 'What happened to those dreams?' she asked softly.

Scrooge's expression was grim and he did not reply. A few seconds later they were flying through the air again. They hovered outside a window, and then passed right through it.

Fan and Young Ebenezer were listening to a lawyer reading their father's will.

'*And so, because of my daughter's foolhardiness, I leave all my money and estates to my son, Ebenezer. Signed, James Scrooge.*' The lawyer glanced at Fan. 'I'm sorry, miss.'

Fan burst into tears, and ran from the room.

'My father never approved of her marriage to Frederic,' Scrooge explained.

'And Fan died, giving birth to her baby, did she not?' the ghost asked in a grating voice.

Scrooge nodded. 'My nephew, Fred.'

The ghost lifted her cone, and began to spin again. Magically, the whole scene changed in a blur to the bright colours of autumn.

'What was I supposed to do?' Scrooge demanded. 'Should I have shared my father's money with that good-for-nothing husband of hers?'

The ghost did not answer. She looked tired and old and simply pointed to the scene in front of them.

They were in Scrooge's office. Belle sat at the desk, reading a document, while Young Ebenezer stood watching her.

'So this is how you finally propose to me!' Belle said angrily. 'With a *business* contract?'

Young Ebenezer cleared his throat. 'Surely you can see that our positions are . . . very different?'

Scrooge turned away as if he couldn't bear to watch. But the ghost touched his face lightly with her glowing finger, forcing him to look again.

'What happened to our dreams, Ebenezer?' Belle asked sadly.

Young Ebenezer shrugged. 'I've not changed towards you, have I?'

Belle stood up. 'Are you sure? What if you met me now – a girl without a penny to her name?'

'I do not make the world we live in, Belle.' Young Ebenezer looked uncomfortable. 'But I am a man of my word.'

Belle looked even sadder. 'I release you from our engagement, Ebenezer,' she said quietly. 'Be happy in the life you have chosen.'

'Say something, damn you!' Scrooge roared. But Young Ebenezer kept silent, even when Belle left the room in tears.

'What happened to those dreams?' the ghost asked again as Young Ebenezer threw the marriage contract into the fire. She looked like an old, old woman; she was no longer the young girl Scrooge had first seen.

Scrooge could stand it no longer. 'NO!' he shouted, and made a desperate grab for the ghost's cone. But the spirit pulled it away easily, and began to spin around him.

'I wish to see no more!' Scrooge moaned as a green mist surrounded him. 'Don't torment me any longer!'

Chapter Eight
The Ghost of Christmas Present

The ghost disappeared in a swirl of green fog. And, to his relief, Scrooge found himself back in his own bedroom at last.

'It is over!' he muttered, collapsing onto the bed. 'And I will carry on leading my life just as I have done. Humbug!'

Gabriel staggered out of the dressing-gown pocket as Scrooge's eyes began to close.

'Humbug!' he muttered again, and began to snore.

Belle's letter lay on the bed. Curious now after what he had seen, Gabriel dragged it out of the envelope and looked at it. Ellen scampered over to see, too.

'I write to you in the hour of my deepest despair. Once we were one in heart. I beg you, Ebenezer ...'

Gabriel dropped the letter and sadly turned away. From what he had seen tonight, Belle had no hope.

'Squeak!' Ellen said, at last understanding why Gabriel was there.

Gabriel told her exactly what he'd seen that night: Scrooge had pushed Belle aside once. It was no good.

Suddenly a bell rang out. A blazing golden light was shining from the living-room, making the whole bedroom glow.

Scrooge sat bolt upright, and stared. 'What now?' he muttered, rolling out of bed. 'If it is a spirit, make yourself known!'

'Come in and know me better!' boomed a cheerful voice.

Scrooge stumbled over to the door and into the golden light. Gabriel and Ellen followed him.

The dark, dreary living-room was transformed. Holly and ivy garlands were hanging on the walls, and every surface was groaning with huge platters of food – meat, bread, fruit and cheese. In the middle of the feast stood a large, merry-faced man in a long golden robe, with a garland of leaves on his head and a torch in his hand.

'I am the Ghost of Christmas Present,' the spirit announced.

'This had better all be paid for!' Scrooge

snapped. Meanwhile, Gabriel and Ellen had found a plate of pies and begun stuffing themselves happily.

The ghost roared with laughter. 'I come to teach you joy, Mr Scrooge. Joy that makes a banquet out of a simple meal . . .'

In an instant, all the food and decorations vanished into thin air. All Gabriel and Ellen had left was a small pie.

'Joy, Mr Scrooge, that comes from sharing,' the ghost went on.

'I am a simple man, spirit.' For the first time, Scrooge noticed Gabriel, sitting next to Ellen on the cheeseboard. 'I don't ask for charity from others.'

The ghost lifted his glowing torch, and shook a shower of sparkles over Scrooge. Some of them also landed on the two mice. 'We can't afford to waste time,' he boomed. 'I have so much to show you. Touch my robe.'

Scrooge reached out reluctantly. As he did so, Gabriel grabbed the bottom of Scrooge's dressing-gown and, with his other paw, grabbed onto Ellen. As Scrooge and the ghost flew up into the air, Gabriel and Ellen were pulled along with them.

At first they were flying through a haze of

bright sparkles, and then over an icy London street. Children were throwing snowballs at each other, and people were queuing outside the baker's shop. They were carrying their Christmas birds, so that the baker could roast them in his large oven.

'Do you mind, Mr Balcombe!' one man snapped, elbowing his way into the queue.

'Hang on!' Mr Balcombe argued. 'I was here first.'

The ghost smiled. He waved his torch, showering sparkles over the two men.

'You're right,' the first man admitted. 'It *is* Christmas, after all. You go first.'

'No, please, after you,' Mr Balcombe insisted.

Scrooge and the two mice were amazed at the power of the ghost's magic torch. Wherever he shook the sparkles, joy and happiness and Christmas cheer flowed. They flew over a dark, dusty coal mine, and the ghost scattered sparkles over a miner who was trudging wearily home after a hard day's work. The miner's coal-blackened face lit up instantly as his two children came running to meet him.

They flew out over a stormy sea, where a

ship was being tossed around on the waves. The ghost turned and handed the torch to Scrooge. Gabriel looked surprised, but Ellen thought it was a very good idea.

'Does it ever run out?' Scrooge asked, sprinkling sparkles over the sailors below.

'Not for the present,' the ghost replied.

On they flew, over a lighthouse, a church, a large mansion. Smiling, Scrooge scattered the sparkles of Christmas happiness over all the people they met.

'Come,' the ghost said urgently, taking the torch back, 'we don't have much time.'

The ghost guided Scrooge down onto a rooftop. They passed through it into a dining-room, where the table was laid for Christmas dinner. In the drawing-room next door, a merry crowd of people were gathered.

Scrooge's nephew, Fred, was standing in the middle of the room. He was counting a pile of coins, staring at them very intently.

'Is it animal, vegetable or mineral, Fred?' a woman asked.

'He can't answer that, dear,' her husband replied. 'He can only say "yes" or "no". That's the game.'

'Is it animal, Fred?' asked his wife, Alice.

'Yes!' Fred nodded.

'Is it a duck with one leg?' asked a man called Topper, and everyone laughed, including Scrooge.

'Is it an old goat?' enquired one of the other women.

'I know!' Alice exclaimed suddenly. 'It's Uncle Scrooge!'

'Yes!' Fred laughed. 'You've got it!'

Scrooge looked taken aback.

'I was right when I said "old goat", then!' laughed the other woman. 'I win!'

Gabriel thought that was very amusing, but Ellen didn't.

'It's hard to believe that old tightfist is your uncle, Fred!' Topper grinned.

'Well, he *is* a mean old so-and-so,' Fred agreed. 'I asked him to dinner tonight, but he said no.'

'Enough of that dreadful skinflint,' Alice said firmly. 'Come and sit at the table.'

Scrooge grasped the ghost's sleeve. 'Is this what people *really* think of me?' he asked sadly.

The laughter of the party followed them as they drifted outside.

'No respect!' Scrooge went on bitterly.

'Squanderers! Forever spending money they don't have!'

'Your nephew reaches out to you,' the ghost said gravely as they flew over a busy London street. 'He has your sister's heart.'

'He hasn't an ounce of common sense!' Scrooge snapped. 'He should never have got married, until—'

He stopped as the ghost drew to a halt, hovering above the street.

'What's going on here?' Scrooge asked curiously. 'What is this to do with me?'

'A Merry Christmas from Mr Scrooge!' yelled a mocking voice below them.

Old Joe and his men were loading furniture onto a wagon. A woman and child stood watching them. Both were crying. The woman's husband dashed forward to try and stop the men, but Joe pushed him aside.

'And don't fall behind on your payments again!' he roared, as the wagon drove off.

Scrooge looked shocked. 'I did not realize . . .' he stammered. 'I don't think you understand how business works. Are *you* a businessman?'

The ghost did not answer that. 'How well do you know Cratchit, your clerk?' he asked.

'Well enough,' Scrooge snapped as they flew down into one of the poorer areas of the city. They stopped outside an old, derelict-looking house and glided through the window.

Mrs Cratchit, Rosy, Peter and Sara were sitting at the Christmas table.

'Look who's here, everybody!' Cratchit came into the room, carrying Tiny Tim.

His wife frowned. 'Bob, he's better off in bed.'

'We can't have Christmas dinner without Tim, dear.' Cratchit put his son gently in a chair as Tim began to cough.

The ghost turned to Scrooge. 'You remember the little boy?'

'No.' Scrooge looked mystified. 'Should I?'

That was too much for Gabriel. He flew at Scrooge, squeaking angrily, and Ellen had to pull him back.

Cratchit stood up, glass in hand. 'Here's to all of us on this splendid Christmas!' he announced. 'And here's to the founder of our feast, Mr Scrooge!'

There was silence, broken only by Tim's coughing.

'Oh, Father!' Sara sighed.

'Mr Scrooge has employed me for fourteen years,' Cratchit went on. 'He has put this bird on our table.'

Mrs Cratchit slammed her fork down on her plate. 'He threw a bucket of cold water over our Tim!' she said furiously. 'I will not toast that mean old man!'

Scrooge hung his head in shame.

'Mr Scrooge didn't *mean* to throw that water at Tim,' Cratchit said gently, as Tim broke into another fit of coughing. 'He just doesn't like Christmas.'

'Will the poor mite live?' Scrooge asked the ghost anxiously.

'What's it to you?' the ghost replied. 'Let him die, and decrease the population!'

'Don't torture me, spirit!' Scrooge cried. 'Tell me the future!'

The ghost moved away. 'I know nothing of the future. I am of the present . . .'

And then he was gone, in a swirl of coloured mist . . .

Chapter Nine
The Ghost of Christmas Future

Silence.

Then, out of the fog, a thin, skeletal finger gradually appeared . . .

'Are you the third spirit?' Scrooge gasped as Gabriel and Ellen leapt out of sight into his pocket.

There was a thunderous roar. A huge skeleton-like figure stood before Scrooge, dressed in a dark robe.

'Tell me!' Scrooge begged, trembling with fear. 'Will that poor boy live?'

The spirit did not speak, but simply raised its arms. The silhouettes of the Cratchit family appeared in front of Scrooge, sitting round their Christmas table.

'Come now, children,' Cratchit was saying bravely, 'Tim would have wanted us to be cheerful.'

'He always loved Christmas,' Sara sighed. 'Especially the snow.'

'He loved to slide,' Cratchit said. 'I'd carry him on my shoulders and—' He broke down.

'Oh!' Scrooge moaned, clutching his head in his hands. 'Are these shades of things to come?'

The spirit loomed over Scrooge without speaking. Another group of people had appeared through the swirl of fog.

'Old Joe?' Scrooge recognized some of them. 'And that's Mother Gimlet, who cleans my house. Why are these people here?'

'I have a right to look after myself,' Mother Gimlet was saying. 'Lord knows, *he* did.'

'True,' agreed one of the other woman.

'I deserve it after the fright he gave me,' Mother Gimlet went on. 'Been lying there dead for three days. No-one knew or cared.'

'Who *would* have cared anyway?' the other woman pointed out. They all laughed, as Mother Gimlet passed some clothes and linen to Joe.

'Nine and six, and not a penny more!' Joe offered. 'What about his bed clothes, and his curtains?'

Scrooge turned to the ghost. 'Does no-one care about this man's death, whoever he might be?'

The swirling fog hid the people from view, as the silent spirit showed Scrooge another scene.

The Alms Hospital. Dr Lambert was holding Belle's hands, and whirling her around joyfully. 'The very best news, Belle!' he cried. 'He's gone! He can no longer bleed us dry!'

Gabriel and Ellen looked at each other, puzzled, as Belle pulled away from the doctor. Her face was sad.

'I don't know whom our debt will be transferred to,' Dr Lambert went on gleefully, 'but he can't be as cruel as Ebenezer Scrooge!'

Shivering violently, Scrooge fell to his knees. There, in front of him was a gravestone. HERE LIES EBENEZER SCROOGE . . .

'Aargh!' Scrooge jumped back. 'Am I past all hope? Can these visions be changed?'

An iron chain flew through the air, and locked itself round Scrooge's waist.

'Come, Ebenezer!' The ghost of Marley was before him. 'You have no time to waste!'

'*Oh!*' Scrooge moaned.

Terrified, Gabriel and Ellen held onto each other tightly.

Bong!

The church bell rang out.

Bong!

The fog was fading . . .

Scrooge opened his eyes. He was lying on his very own bed. 'I – I'm alive!' he stammered in amazement. He reached for Gabriel and Ellen, and danced joyfully around the room with them. 'I'm alive!'

Chapter Ten

Merry Christmas, Mr Scrooge!

Scrooge put the mice down and dashed over to the window. He flung it open and sniffed the cold, crisp air. 'What day is it?' he yelled to a boy who was making a snowman in the street.

'It's Christmas Day, sir,' the boy replied.

'Don't take me for a fool, boy!' Scrooge snapped.

'It is, sir!' the boy insisted. 'Listen to the church bells!'

Scrooge turned away from the window. 'Only one night has passed,' he muttered, dazed. 'It was just a bad dream . . . No! I *must* change. But how?'

'Squeak!' Gabriel tried to help by pointing at the boy.

Scrooge turned and hurried back to the window. 'I didn't mean to snap just now,' he called. 'M-m . . . merry Christmas! Now

66

listen to me carefully.' Scrooge rolled up a banknote, and threw it down to the boy. 'I want you to buy a turkey and a goose – the biggest you can find! And then deliver them to Mr Cratchit of Mabey Street, Camden. Oh, and keep the change!'

The boy looked pleased. He grabbed the banknote, which had landed on the snowman's head, and ran off.

Scrooge was so excited, he danced a jig. 'I must not forget Tiny Tim,' he reminded himself. 'Now . . .' His gaze fell on Ellen and Gabriel, who were standing on the bed next to Belle's letter. 'The letter . . .'

Scrooge picked up the envelope and took the letter out. He grew white as he read it, and his eyes filled with tears. 'Belle, I'm sorry,' he muttered. 'I won't let you down *this* time.'

Scrooge slipped the letter under his robe next to his heart. Then he smiled at the two mice. 'Don't go away!'

He went to the kitchen, and returned with a cake and a large piece of cheese. 'Now, nothing's to be left by the time I return!' he laughed. Gabriel and Ellen were thrilled.

The people out and about in the street were amazed when Scrooge rushed out of his house, shouting, 'Merry Christmas, everyone!' They could hardly believe their eyes and ears. What had got into the miserable old man?

Scrooge danced his way down the street to the fruit-seller and bought a bag of oranges. 'I must not forget Tiny Tim,' he murmured, as he handed out oranges to surprised passersby. 'Merry Christmas!'

'Here's your money, sir.' Looking smug, Old Joe handed Scrooge a bulging bag of coins.

Scrooge took the money bag and glared at him. 'I will not be needing your services again!' he said sternly.

'But – Guv'nor . . . !' Old Joe stammered, looking dismayed.

'And that is final!' Scrooge marched out of the dark alley. He passed the blind beggar and his dog, and dropped the money bag into the beggar's cup.

Scrooge hurried on to the Alms Hospital, but he was much too late. The door had been broken down, and every sick child and every stick of furniture in the place had gone. He was shocked to see exactly what his greed had done. Lost in thought, he made his way home again.

'Ebenezer?' As Scrooge unlocked his door, a voice spoke to him from the shadows.

'Belle!' he exclaimed in delight.

Upstairs, Ellen and Gabriel were just finishing their meal. They heard voices, and raced over to the window.

'Did you ever read my letter?' Belle asked coldly.

'Yes, Belle, I did,' Scrooge replied. 'And I went to the hospital.'

'So you've seen what your men have done!' Belle went on bitterly.

Scrooge hung his head in shame. 'Yes. I was too late.'

Belle looked deep into Scrooge's eyes. 'Why didn't you help me?'

Scrooge broke down. 'I would do anything to change these terrible things!' he sobbed. 'I have so much money. I would be rid of it all, if only I could forget the last twenty years . . .'

Belle's face softened. 'Do you *really* want to change what you have done?'

'It's too late!' Scrooge moaned unhappily.

'No, it's not too late,' Belle argued. 'The

hospital needs you. I need you, Ebenezer. You have so much to give.'

She touched Scrooge gently. Gabriel and Ellen shook hands and then gave each other a big hug.

Bong!

'Oh no!' Cratchit raced down the street, panting hard. 'Not today of all days!'

He ran up the office stairs as fast as he could. Scrooge was waiting for him in the doorway, Gabriel and Ellen sitting on his shoulder.

'Do you know what time it is, Mr Cratchit?' Scrooge snapped.

'Sorry, Mr Scrooge,' Cratchit gasped. 'I was making rather merry yesterday.' He blinked at Gabriel and Ellen. 'Sir, there are two mice—'

'Never mind the mice!' Scrooge said testily. 'They were here on time!' He glared at his assistant. 'I'm not going to stand for it any more, Cratchit!'

His clerk looked frightened. 'Please, sir, it's only once a year,' he stammered. 'I'll make it up, sir.'

'No, Mr Cratchit!' Scrooge snapped. Then his face broke into a beaming smile. 'I shall make it up to *you*! I'm quadrupling your salary as of today! Happy Christmas, Bob!'

Cratchit looked at his boss as if he'd gone mad.

'You can have Marley's office,' Scrooge went on merrily. 'We'll get you an assistant! And I promise to help out your family in every way I can.'

Cratchit was so dazed by his good fortune, he hardly knew what to say.

'Make up the fires, Bob!' Scrooge called cheerfully. 'Scrooge and Cratchit, or Cratchit and Scrooge? What do you think?'

'Did you say *quadruple*, sir?' Cratchit managed to ask.

Dickens looked round at his audience. They were spellbound by his tale, and had hardly made a sound all evening.

'Scrooge was better than his word,' Dickens went on. 'He did it all, and more. He kept Christmas in his heart all through the year, and he was a second father to Tiny Tim, who did *not* die.' The famous author smiled.

'And Gabriel? Well, Gabriel moved to the New World, where he gave a lady sitting in the front row of the theatre the fright of her life!'

71

'Squeak!' Gabriel added.

'And with him came an old friend.' Dickens nodded at Ellen. 'Because who wants to spend their life alone? And that, ladies and gentlemen, is the story of "A Christmas Carol". Not quite the same one I wrote in the book, I admit, but I hope you have enjoyed it.' He smiled at the audience. 'And now I leave you with memories of ghosts past, ghosts present and ghosts yet to come!'

The audience rose to their feet, cheering and applauding loudly. Dickens took a bow as Gabriel and Ellen kissed each other. Then the two mice ran off up the aisle to start their new life in the New World together.

THE END

About Charles Dickens

Born in Portsmouth in 1812, the son of a clerk in the Navy pay office, Charles Dickens had a childhood that alternated between happiness – his early boyhood in Chatham – to real misery, when his father was imprisoned for debt and he had to work in a blacking warehouse, sticking labels on bottles. It is probable that these hardships in his early life had a strong influence on the kind of books he wrote later in life.

Determined to improve himself, he worked as an office boy, then became a reporter of debates in the House of Commons for a newspaper. He began writing articles about London life for a number of newspapers and magazines and his first book, *Pickwick Papers*, was published in 1836 when he was only twenty-five years old. The book first appeared in monthly instalments and his next two books, *Oliver Twist* and *Nicholas Nickleby* were also first in print as monthly episodes.

He wrote a great many books over the following years and *A Christmas Carol* was first published in 1843, his first Christmas story (he had been commissioned to write a Christmas story every year for five years), and the most successful. Several of his books have been filmed – *Oliver Twist*, *Nicholas Nickleby*, *Great Expectations* and *David Copperfield* among them – and *Oliver Twist* was also adapted into the successful stage production *Oliver!*

The Artful Dodger, Pip, Little Nell and – of course – Scrooge will always be immediately recognized as being characters from Dickens' books, many of which have been studied at school by several generations of schoolchildren, and it is probably fair to say that no other writer has ever captured the public imagination in quite the same way that Dickens did. 'Dickensian' has, in fact, become a word used to describe the kind of settings and characters he often portrayed in his novels.

He died, suddenly, in 1870, leaving unfinished his last novel, *The Mystery of Edwin Drood*.

THE GIANT GOLDFISH ROBBERY
Richard Kidd

Forget Moby Dick . . . Forget the great, white whale . . . These were the great orange whales. A whole pondful!

Moving home has not been much fun for Jimmy and his family, least of all for his fisherman father who has had to leave behind the sea and his treasured boat.

Then, out of the blue, Jimmy meets Major Gregory, an elderly gentleman and prize collector of koi carp. Soon Jimmy is hooked and wants to learn everything there is to know about these gentle orange giants. But before long he finds himself in deep – and very dangerous – water.

SHORTLISTED FOR BRANFORD
BOASE AWARD 2000

'The best adventure story for seven-to-ten-year-olds so far this year' *Literary Review*

'A witty contemporary adventure story'
Financial Times

ISBN 0440 86412 7

I WAS A RAT!
Philip Pullman

'I was a RAT!'

So insists Roger. Maybe it's true.
But what is he *now*?
A terrifying monster rampaging in the sewers?
The *Daily Scourge* is sure of it.
A money-spinning fairground freak?
He is to Mr Tapscrew.
A champion wriggler and a downy card?
That's what Billy hopes.
Or just an ordinary small boy, though a little
ratty in his habits?

Only three people believe this version of the
story. Only one of them knows who Roger really
is. And luckily a story about *her* can sell even
more newspapers than one about a rat-boy . . .

'All life is here in this skilful unfolding of a
very human tale from a great storyteller'
Bookseller

'An extraordinary story finely balancing
good and evil, humour and despair,
adventure and parody'
Junior Education

'Combining elements of fairy-tale, satire,
slapstick humour and suspenseful
melodrama . . . a glorious tale'
Guardian

ISBN 0440 863759

THE DREAM MASTER
Theresa Breslin

*'There are always rules . . . I am the Dream Master.
Not you. What I say goes. And I say this dream
is gone, so beat it.'*

There are good dreams and there are rotten
dreams, but once they're over, they're over. Or
are they? For one morning, as Cy is about to
wake up from a terrific dream about Ancient
Egypt, he discovers that he *can* get back into his
dream world. There's just one problem; the
Dream Master, who isn't used to stroppy boys
standing up to him and wanting to break all
the rules. And as Cy moves back and forth
between the present day and the land of the
pharaohs – sorting out all kinds of problems
with schoolwork and bullies – dream life and
real life become ingeniously intertwined!

**'Engaging fantasy . . . treads assuredly the line
between thrills and laughs'**
The Observer

ISBN 0440 863821

GHOST TO THE RESCUE
Helen Dunwoodie

'Aye, lassies! To the rescue!'

That's the cry of Lady Maisie McNeill. She's
been a ghost for two centuries and her
powers are beginning to fade but she's got
one last challenge to meet . . .

Rowan and Bryony Durwood, the 'lassies' in
question, need all the help they can get. Their
favourite wee dog has plunged into a swirling
river, a mysterious American boy has dived
in after the dog and it's all happening in
the middle of their mother's wedding!

Praise for the first book about Lady Maisie,
Ghost on the Loose!:

'A stylish and funny tale'
The Times

**'The narrative moves at a fast pace,
humorously keeping the reader
wound up in events'**
Scotland on Sunday

ISBN 0440 864216